Hot for the
BARTENDER

ALEXANDRIA GONCALVES

Hot for the Bartender

Published by Alexandria Goncalves

Copyright © 2022 by Alexandria Goncalves

All rights reserved.

Cover Design: Emily Witting Designs

Editor: Nisha Ladlee, Nisha's Books and Coffee

This is a work of fiction. Names, characters, places, brands, media, and incidents are either the products of the author's imagination or are used fictitiously. The author acknowledges the trademarked status and trademark owners of various products referenced in this work of fiction, which have been used without permission. The publication/use of these trademarks is not authorized, associated with, or sponsored by the trademark owners.

Life always offers you a second chance. It's called tomorrow.

— DYLAN THOMAS

BLURB

When the woman I once loved walks into my bar, the life I've built is shattered.

I fled everything I've ever known for a small town, forced to run from the motorcycle club I considered family after a deal gone wrong.

After thirty years of laying low, my past has caught up to me in the gorgeous, green-eyed form of Roxanne Archer.

She was my world back then. One look at her now, wearing that crest I once wore with pride, and it all comes rushing back. Everything we had… and how I ruined it all.

But I'm not running this time. I've been given a second chance, and I'll do whatever it takes to make her mine.

DEDICATION

This book is dedicated to my hometown. We've had our ups and our downs, but you helped inspire my writing, and for that, I'm grateful.

PROLOGUE
JOE

I tuck a piece of hair behind Rox's ear, gripping the side of her neck, my thumb caressing her cheek, as I thrust upwards into her wet cunt. No matter how many times we've done it, it always feels like the first time.

Like we were made for one another.

"I see that sappy look in your eyes, Joe." She smiles playfully as she runs her fingers through my shoulder length hair while continuing the slow movement of her hips.

"I'm always going to have this sappy look in my eyes when I'm looking at you, old lady." I wink at her and she leans down to bite my nipple, making me groan.

"You don't get to call me an old lady, until there is a ring on my finger." She throws her wild black locks over her shoulder and quickens her pace on my cock. Feeling my balls tighten, I grab a hold of her hips, aggressively pushing her down on my cock. She begins to whimper as I take control of her body. My girl never has been able to stay in control for too long, she likes being controlled more. I bite my lip as I watch her. Her face in ecstasy. She scrunches her eyes telling me she's almost there. Her pouty lips open slightly, her skin aglow.

She's breathtaking.

Feeling the familiar tightness in my balls again, I bring my thumb to her clit to get her here with me. I slam her down one last time, as she yells fuck. That's my sign and I release with her, my abs tightening and the feeling of weightlessness coming.

I shuffle our bodies so I'm now sitting up against the window of my truck with her straddling me, I grab her face, bringing it softly to mine for a kiss.

The California sunset is behind her, giving her the look of a goddess – my goddess.

"What are you thinking?" She runs her hand along my jawline.

"About how beautiful you are, more beautiful than the sunset behind you." I shrug shamelessly. She turns her body slightly to look at the sunset and gasps.

"You know what? It never gets old. I could turn around every night and seeing the sunset will always bring this warm feeling." She admits, while watching the sun slowly descend into the horizon.

"One day, I'll marry you under the sunset." I admit and she whips around and glares at me with a smile.

"Don't say things you don't mean, Joe." She goes to poke me, but I grab her finger and bring her close to my face,

"I mean every fucking word, Rox. I'll marry you under every sunset, as long as I get to see this look on your face forever." I bring our lips together in a whisper, smiling when she pushes them together for a passionate kiss. If anyone heard me talk to Rox at the club, they would say I'm pussy-whipped. I don't care though, this woman with her long dark hair, stunning green eyes, and infectious personality is my everything. I'd do anything to protect and love her and everyone knows that. I've made my intention with her very clear in front of everyone at the club. I even broke one of my brother's fingers for looking too long at Rox's ass while she was walking to her Dad's office. The perk of being in a motorcycle club is that most things are forgivable, so when someone looks at something that's mine, they should expect brutality. Luckily we're good now, but it showed everyone in the club not to look or touch what's mine.

While Rox looks like a Greek goddess, she's got fire. I'm the only one who gets to see this fire ninety percent of the time, but when something heats her up, there isn't anyone who can put that fire out. She almost stabbed a member once for making a jab at me, but her dad walked out just in time. If it's not me, it's her dad she'll listen to. He's the president of the club and he accepted me into the club without a problem after being a prospect for less than a year. I showed my loyalty to the club, I didn't really have anything else to live for. They became my family, and Rox became my everything.

It's been the best years of my life, and being in the club, I found a place I can call home. Maybe not so much a place, but a person.

I joined on a whim a few years ago, becoming a prospect for just a short period of time. It was only short because there wasn't much that I wouldn't do and our president liked that about me. Does he abuse his power sometimes? Yes – but I'm always the first one ready to take on the action without hesitation. I didn't join a brotherhood to stand around. I joined to find a family and work, my relationship with Rox was a welcoming surprise. I was only a few months into being a prospect when I saw some guys harassing her on her way to the club. I'd seen her around a few times, but hadn't spoken to her. That was my bad boy moment of shine. I pulled my bike over beside her, hopped off, and held a knife to the guy's throat. Not only did that shut him up quick, but it made Rox look at me like her knight in shining armor. I've spent five years living up to that title because she's worth it.

I grab her and smirk as I watch her pull her rose covered dress down to mid-thigh.

"Why are you covering up that sweet body?" I practically whine as I play with the hem of her dress. I brought her up to the cliffside to watch the sunset because I know how much she loves it.

"I'm covering up because you caught me in a moment of lust and I can't be caught naked in the bed of a truck." She fluffs her curls and leans back in-between my legs. I laugh and wrap my arms around her because she's not wrong. We had come into the bed of the truck to cuddle and watch the sunset, but I had her naked and moaning my name in less than five minutes.

I move her hair away from her neck and place a small kiss there as we face the sun. The sky has officially darkened, but the blue-pink hues are still prominent in the sky.

I watch the irises of her eyes get bigger as she watches the hues take up the sky. It's a breathtaking moment. I can see the reflection of colors in her eyes, and I feel this fullness in my chest that comes whenever we're alone. "Forever," I whisper as I lower my head into the crook of her neck. I don't have to watch the sunset to be mesmerized when I have this woman in my arms.

CHAPTER ONE
JOE

Thirty years later…

"What's the point of having workers, if they don't listen to a damn thing you say?" I grumble to myself as I haul cases of beer into the fridge in the back of the bar. I need to get four kegs, at least, into the bar for tonight. Running out of booze on a night where my bar is full of bikers isn't going to work. Lifting a couple more boxes, I'm feeling the strain in my arms pulling. I'm not a big guy but I throw my weight around in the gym every now and then to make sure I stay in shape and the pain is evident today. I force myself to keep putting stuff away, regardless of my arms feeling like they're going to go limp any second now. I grab the final box and stack it on the last case of Stella Artois that's leaning against the far right wall. Taking a step back, I realize my back room looks like a rainbow of booze. From the beer cases that stack along the bottom, to the shelves of various alcohol, it's a sight to see.

Walking out of the fridge, I glance around, at least the kitchen staff cleared the space. The smell of grease is pretty pungent since I decided to have a Thursday wing night for the Toronto Geese game. Victoria, Auston, Emma, and Hannah came by and it was a good night for a Thursday. They're all off for the summer due to their teaching positions and Auston has been helping his dad during the odd times. They've been around a lot more and it's made things more bearable. I swear the older I get, the more I think about the past. It's like a fucking nagging old lady that never goes away. I snicker to myself at the thought because I figured by now I would have myself an old lady – but the universe had different ideas in place for my life. I'm not mad with the way my life turned out, I'm actually grateful I got out when I did because most likely, I would've been six feet under by now.

Lifting up the last keg of beer that I need from the back room, I maneuver my way around to the front of the bar to connect it to the tap. With the summer crowd starting to kick up, I've been ordering more and more kegs of beer due to all the students coming home from college. Today is special though, because it's Friday the 13th. To the locals, it's a regular day that bikers come from all over North America to spend time in a nearby town with fellow bikers. It reminds me of my old life, the one I had before I was forced to leave.

The familiar rumble of bikes passing brings me comfort. I stopped riding as soon as I moved here. I felt like I needed to disconnect from my previous life as much as I could. Buying the bar was the closest familiarity I could get to without giving anyone any idea of who I am. I moved here thirty years ago, so the odds of someone knowing who I am would be slim. Moving from California to a small town in southern Ontario, I knew I didn't have much to worry about.

I swing through the door to the bar and come to a halt. There's a woman sitting at the bar, but it isn't just any woman. She's got a leather jacket on, with a familiar crest for "Devils Rejects" covering the back. Her long hair peppered with gray draped in waves down her back. Suddenly, the weight of this keg feels like it's tripled as I stare at her back.

It can't be.

I feel like time has frozen. I remember a moment exactly like this one, but I was walking to meet her for our first date – and we're twenty-one years old at that time.

Thirty years have passed now.

"Are you just going to just stand there, Joe?" Her voice hasn't changed at all in the time we've been apart. My feet finally function and the only sound is my boots on the concrete floor.

I set the keg under the bar with my back to her. Taking a deep breath, I finally turn around to see if this is true, or if I'm just seeing a mirage from my past.

It's like time never passed, those same sparkling green eyes stare back at me. However, they aren't filled with the love they once had. Right now there's betrayal, hurt, and anger found within them.

"Roxanne, what are you doing here?" I question, taking her in. She's aged slightly; some wrinkles on her forehead, the sprinkle of gray and black in her hair, but she's still the most beautiful woman I've ever laid my eyes on. The conflicting emotions fill my chest with unease as I get a look at her, like a weighted pressure of both fear and love.

"Don't you fucking 'Roxanne, what are you doing here?' me. It's been thirty years, Joe. Thirty years since I've seen you or even heard from you. I didn't even know if you were still alive." Her voice cracks towards the end and I lower my head in shame. The one person I loved with all my heart – I left.

No explanation, nothing.

On the terms that I left on, I was out bad. I left the club without giving them any idea of it, and with a myriad of problems to deal with. Were the problems started by me? No, but disappearing out of the blue put a large target on my back. We have charters all over the world, and I've been lucky enough to go this long without being caught.

Well, until now.

I take a deep breath and look back up at her, "what do you want me to say, Rox?" I say resigned. I lean my arms on the bar and I catch her eyes go to my tattooed arms flexing against the grip I have on the countertop.

The fire is still there. I see it in her eyes, but it's quickly burned away when she looks back up at me.

"I want to know what the fuck happened? Why'd you disappear and land in this little bumpkin town in Canada?" She straightens her back.

The bar isn't open yet, but I must have forgotten to lock the doors behind me. My mind was full of everything I had to do before the afternoon came and bikers filled my bar.

"I fucked up, alright?" I pause. I haven't thought about this day in over thirty years. I saw stuff no fucking twenty-one year old should see, but it came with the territory. I take a deep breath because I know I need to admit everything that's happened. I'm tired of the lies and guilt that has consumed me all these years. "Your dad fucking lied to me. He sent me off to kill someone, who he vaguely described as someone who did something wrong to our rivals, the Streetwolves. Not wanting to destroy our alliance with them – I did it – no questions asked. However, your dad never told me I was killing one of the most powerful drug lords on the west coast." I grumble, my eyes becoming slits automatically. I run my hand through my dark peppered hair and move back to lean my body on the bar behind me, crossing my arms.

"The reason I didn't come back? I got caught by one of his men. I was tortured for weeks to give up information on the Devil's Rejects and Streetwolves." I lean my head back towards the ceiling, "and I did."

I'll never forget that moment, being locked in between four concrete walls for weeks on end. They tortured me in every way possible, without leaving any permanent damage. I mean, I have plenty of scars to show from my past, but they're covered with tattoos. I had plenty of scars already when I was a part of the club, but the only way to cover the multitude of them that covered my body was with more tattoos. From my collarbones down – I'm covered. I'd been cut by a machete and various knives, but there was no pain like the one in my chest. The deepest scar lays over my heart from when I left Roxanne, but I had no choice.

At my weakest moment, I gave in.

I was let go as soon as I'd given up all five years worth of information I had about the Devil's Rejects. As soon as I felt the sunlight beam down on my raw skin, I hightailed it out of California, out of the US.

Without looking back, I left because I knew if I went back to the clubhouse and they found out what I did, I'd be killed without a thought.

It was the hardest decision I had ever made in my life, but Rox's dad not being completely honest with me fucked that all up. I was reckless in my twenties. If I knew stacks of cash was coming in from a job, I would do it, no question asked. If I would've known who I was killing, I'd have gone in with a better plan. However, our President, Jack, Rox's dad, under-played how much exactly we were being paid. Clearly something shady was taking place. While I sat in that dingy place being tortured, I realized my one way out was betraying the club I had honored for five years, forcing me to leave the country.

CHAPTER TWO

ROX

I see the pain in his eyes, and I try not to care, but my heart twists in agony. He left me, when he promised me the world, and left me in a burning one.

After years of anger, I'd finally lashed out at my dad. The president of the Devil's Rejects. I became no better than him with hatred filling my veins. When I found out that Joe had disappeared, I thought he was killed. I spent years trying to figure out what the fuck happened to him. I hurt anyone who got in my way of trying to find out, but I always ended up in the same place I started.

The clubhouse.

My dad had used my anger to his advantage making me the perfect weapon in the clubhouse. Everyone feared me; whether it was my use of seduction, or my way around a knife, everyone on the West Coast feared me.

They knew who I was. I was well-known by different gangs on the West Coast because I was known for getting the job done successfully and feared if my anger got the best of me.

I was never like this though. I used to be the girl who

dreamed she would get out, with Joe, and run away to live our lives the way we wanted. I wore floral dresses, was naïve, and believed positivity was the best medicine. However, he fucked that all up and left me with a huge mess and a narcissistic angry president.

"You should have come back to the club and told us." I grind out, gripping the edge of the bar in a white-knuckle force.

"I should have come to the club?" He asks ludicrously, a bewildered look in his eyes. "You and I both know I would have been skinned alive the moment I let everyone know what I did."

"Well, I'm glad you got away fucking scot-free. I had to clean up your mess, and while doing so lost who I was." I shout at him while standing up. Anger vibrates between both of us, his eyes in slits.

I'm about to throw the chair in front of me at him, when he suddenly makes his way towards me, around the bar.

"Scotch fucking free, really Rox? I left my life, because your father cared more about fucking dollar signs than he did *his* club." He shouts in my face. "I've spent the last thirty years – alone. In a fucking country where I didn't know a soul, away from everything I love." He growls at me and I can't help feel the familiar intense build that used to occur when we fought. It happened sometimes when we were in our late teens. We both had passion within us, and it often got out of hand, and we'd fuck wherever we were. We didn't care about our actions or getting caught.

"I'm not going to pity you, Joe. You knew what you were doing when you told the cartel everything." I push my shoulders back, to feign confidence, a mere foot between us. Although I told him I won't pity him, a small part of me does.

It's hard to come face to face with the emotions built up over thirty years.

He lets out a harsh laugh. "I knew what I was doing? Fuck Rox, you're not naïve. I was going to be killed regardless, they tortured me for two weeks. You know better than anyone else what happens when we're caught. I saved myself." There it is. The familiar fire in his eyes, I thought it was gone. When I walked in here, I sensed how he had become soft. The ache and sadness was evident in his eyes, but I wanted – no, needed – to know the fire was still there.

That my Joe was still there, even though I wanted to carve his fucking heart out.

I see the sudden dullness in his eyes, his new rise of softness coming back to his senses and I don't waste a second.

I grab his face and bring his lips to mine. I'm so angry with how soft he has become, and want to bring the fire back. The fear that the passion we once had no longer being there makes my heart drop. As soon as our lips touch though, I feel like I'm twenty again. Nothing feels like it's changed, but everything has.

My heart weeps at the years we've spent apart. As much as the anger has consumed me all these years, the sadness hurts more. I've missed the feeling of his lips on mine, his arms wrapped around me protectively, and the utter possessiveness that used to hold him when I was concerned.

Joe picks me up and I wrap my legs around his waist as he sets my jean clad ass on the bar. We battle for dominance, but in the end, I soften against him. Nothing has changed. I still like him in control and it makes me sigh internally.

I reach down and lean away from him to throw my shirt backwards behind the bar.

"Fuck Rox, you're just as beautiful as I remember," he mumbles as he leans down to trail kisses along the top of my breasts. I shiver, my nipples turning rough against the black bra I'm wearing.

"I need you to fuck me, Joe. I need you to put all those years of anger into me. Right. Now." I growl, to refrain my real emotions from bubbling.

It's like I unleash a beast because Joe leans back and grabs ahold of my bra and rips it in the middle, my breasts bounce from the release. He reaches behind his neck and grabs his shirt from behind and I watch him like some love sick puppy that's never seen a man take his shirt off before. He's mesmerizing.

He's also fucking ripped. When I walked in here, I was expecting a man with a beer belly and a lost look in his eyes. I didn't expect to find a jacked, tattooed, blue eyed fox.

"Oh my God..." I stare in awe at the tattoos that now cover his body. Before my eyes make it back to his, he's undoing the button of my jeans and pushing them down my legs.

"Fuck, you're still going commando?" He groans out and I laugh. The first real laugh I've had in a long time. He shakes his head as he lowers his mouth and blows a cool breath onto my cunt.

I bite my lip to keep from moaning as he uses his left hand to pull my lips apart, his eyes lighting up.

His tongue dives down and strokes along my pussy, making me groan loudly. He continues his feast on my core, like I'm the first meal that he's had in years. Leaning my elbows back on the bar, I watch him, completely hypnotized. His facial hair is glistening with my juices and another pang of arousal stirs deep within me.

"Fuck, Joe..." I turn my head to the side and it's as if me moaning his name has triggered something. He really begins to devour me then and I bend my legs up on the bar, grabbing ahold of his hair. "Fuck, fuck, fuck." I repeat loudly as the crescendo of an orgasm begins to tingle in my toes.

My head falls back and my whole body tightens as I let go. Joe doesn't hesitate to lick up all my juices as they drip from me.

He slowly rises, looking like a fallen king, and doesn't break eye contact as I hear the clang of him undoing his pants.

I'm the first to break our eye contact as my gaze slowly makes its way down his body, towards his hard cock. I smile, as I see he never covered it up.

He begins to run the tip of his cock through my wet lips and I look back up at him through hooded eyes.

"What? You thought I would have it covered?" His head tilts to the side. "Never." With that he pushes his entire length straight into me. Lurching forward, I lean up to grab ahold of his shoulders. He wraps his arms around me and quickens his pace. I run my nails along his back and he releases a hiss of pleasure.

Some things don't change.

I keep my ankles locked around his thighs and kiss along his neck as he keeps thrusting into me.

"Fuck Rox, I won't last long." He mumbles as he stares up at the ceiling and I let out a huff of laughter.

"Did you ever?" I question, using my hands to bring his face back towards mine.

"Never with you." He leans forward and takes my bottom lip between his teeth and adds a little pressure before sucking it into his mouth. I moan awkwardly with my lip in his mouth. My pussy clenches, and I begin to feel another orgasm coming.

"Give it to me, Joe." He begins to pound harder, gripping

15

me like I might disappear and I swear I can feel him all the way in my throat.

Holy fuck.

My orgasm breaches and I let it all go. My body tightens around his and he roars out as he comes in me. I'm not worried that we didn't use a condom, I still take birth control, and my period ending days are near.

The pressure from what just happened is overwhelming.

I feel tears begin to flood and as much as I want to hide them, I can't. For the first time in thirty years, I allow myself to feel the emotions I've been holding back.

Thirty years – it's been thirty years since I've been able to hold the only man I've ever loved. The man I thought fell off the face of the earth, for all these years.

I keep my head in the crook of Joe's neck and bite my lip to keep a sob from breaking out. As if he knows, he lifts his head and grabs mine, to bring our faces together.

"Rox…" He draws out, sadly. He picks me up and carries me somewhere. I have no idea where but I keep my head resting on his shoulder, trying to get a hold of my emotions. I'm fifty years old for fuck sake, I shouldn't be crying this hard over a man.

Except he wasn't just any man… he was my everything.

CHAPTER THREE
JOE

I'm in disbelief over what just happened, but I can't deny the brief happiness I'm feeling over it. Being inside Rox reminded me of exactly who we were in the past. But we're thirty years older and a lot of things have changed.

I carry her up the stairs to my apartment above the bar, shoving the door open with my foot, and make my way to the bed to set her down. I tuck her into my bed as I quickly grab a bottle of water for her from the fridge in the kitchen. I grab a pair of jeans from the couch and walk back into my room,

"I got you some water in case you're thirsty." I hand her the bottle and she shuffles her body so she's leaning against the headboard. I sit down, placing my hand on her thigh as I watch her glance around my space.

There isn't much in my bedroom. I've got a black king bed with two matching dressers, and a leather seat in the corner. I don't spend much time here, between the gym and the bar, my apartment is mainly for sleep. After leaving California, I felt completely alone, so being in a people dominated workplace helped keep me busy.

"I'm not complaining, but Rox, how did you find me?"

She huffs out a laugh, letting her head thud back against the headboard. She closes her eyes for a brief moment before she opens them again. They are watery again, but now behind them all I see is anger.

"There's a lot you don't know, Joe." She says sadly and my face twists in confusion. I'm sure there are a lot of things that I've missed out on over the years, but I can't allow myself to have any regrets because I probably wouldn't be here if it wasn't for the decisions I made.

I grab her hand in mine, looking down at it before saying, "What do you mean, Rox? Be straight with me, you know I've never enjoyed having to drag answers out." I watch her eyes shift slightly and I've never seen her so uncomfortable. Her shoulders are tight and she squeezes my hand that's now resting on her thigh.

"The week before you had that job," she pauses to take a deep breath, "I found out I was pregnant." My eyes widen in shock and my stomach twists.

I take my hand out of hers and drag it down my face before I stand up abruptly. All these years, I've had a kid? My chest constricts with something I've never felt. They must hate me, thinking that I abandoned their mother when she needed me most, when they both did. I run my hand through my hair and look at her, but there is grief written all over her face.

"What…" I'm in disbelief, but Rox's eyes are filled with fresh tears ready to spill over again.

"My dad made me abort it. I aborted it a week after you were sent on that job with the cartel because my dad had made up a story that you died." She breaks and I'm speechless. I knew her dad was a piece of shit because I'd seen him do some shady stuff in his life, but I never expected him to want his own grandchild dead, or me for that matter.

Rox wipes her fingers under her eyes to try and collect herself and the tears that don't seem to stop falling from her eyes. I can feel the pain radiating from her and I take a deep breath, realizing this isn't just about me.

This is about Rox too, the hurt she had to feel with me leaving her behind when I promised her I never would, and then losing our child to top it all off.

"Dad died two weeks ago, but I don't want to get into that now. For the past thirty years, I've been filled with so much hatred and so much anger for letting him use me as his pawn again and again." She shakes her head, everything she's gone through being at the forefront. I know because I've been there before. The disgust we feel internally, even though it wasn't our fault. We were put in unbeatable situations.

"When he died, I felt relieved. So much fucking relief. I told our VP I was leaving, and I wasn't coming back. But before doing that, I went into his office at the clubhouse a week later. I planned to burn everything until I found a box that had your name written in tiny letters in the top left. He kept it hidden under four other boxes for a reason, clearly." She pauses again to take a sip of water and I feel like I'm being tortured all over again. I'm finding out things I never thought I would. I thought I would spend the rest of my days in this bar – never having to confront the ghosts of my past – until the day I die:

"I opened the box immediately, hoping to fuck that it was about you and not some other person. When I opened it, I found everything from the past thirty years. I mean, there wasn't much – you've been here for thirty years. But when I found out where you lived, that you owned a bar, and sold your bike – your most cherished item – I knew it was my sign to come and find you. I know I came in here guns blazing with anger, but really, I just needed to know you were okay.

My dad made me think you were killed. I didn't want to believe him, so I made myself believe you just left me." She sobs and I just want to hold her. Grabbing a hold of her again, I bring her towards me, wrapping my arms around her. I had no idea that her father had done any of this. I didn't know he had been tracking me for thirty years, which is unsettling because I thought I was doing a good job at hiding. But I also didn't realize that Rox had been through hell. From losing our kid, to thinking I left her or worse, died, to having to go thirty years in the club alone doing god knows what... I can't stomach it. The guilt I feel right now is like nothing I've ever felt. I could have tried to contact her over the past thirty years but I was scared. I was scared any form of contact I had would somehow put my life in jeopardy.

We sit in silence for what feels like an hour, just holding one another. She cries quietly and I leave her alone to come down from the emotional high and allow her to feel my presence.

My sadness for everything that happened is overwhelming. I shoved my feelings into a box, hoping I would never have to come face to face with them again but she's here and now I feel like shit. I don't know how I'll ever be able to make it up to her. Anyone else from our past would have walked through my bar doors and killed me. I'm not sure what happened to the club after I left, too afraid if I somehow tried to look – someone would find me.

Rox went through hell though. My girl with the fiery passion hidden beneath beautiful long hair and a floral print dress became a hard-hearted woman who clearly has the guilt of her past on her shoulders.

"I'm so sorry," I say after what feels like forever. "I don't know what I can do, or say, that would make your pain go away, Rox." I cup her face with both hands and look her in the eyes. The green shimmers from all the tears shed, and her face is a little puffy, but she looks like she's lifted a weight that's been on her shoulders for years.

"I…" She takes a shuddered breath, "I just wanted to see you." She runs her finger tips along my lips and I nip at them. I want to bring the smile back to her face. Since she's gotten here, we've gone through some lifelong weighted emotions. I need to see that smile I fell in love with so long ago. I know *that* Rox is in there.

"Let me take you somewhere?" I pose this as a question because I have no idea if she even wants to stay here after seeing me. After all, she did just say she wanted to *see* me. Clearly, we've done a little more than that…

"Okay." She nods and I pull the blanket back and grab her hand to help her up. She follows me back down the stairs and I grab the bar keys from the little hook by my door to the apartment.

"You can take my bike." She says behind me and I stop. I haven't been on a bike since I arrived here. I sold my bike to help pay rent for the space above the bar when I first got here. Luckily, a bar in a small town can be successful and I ended up buying the whole building around fifteen years ago. However, I never stepped foot back on a bike.

"Really?" I ask her, not able to help the excitement. For fifty years old, I feel like a kid in a candy shop, because the feeling of riding a bike is like no other. Rox lets go of my hand and jogs over behind the bar to grab her jacket and clothes that were thrown recklessly behind it while we were having sex. She pulls the keys out of the jacket and dangles them in front of me and I snatch them, the excitement hitting me full force.

She's about to shrug her jacket on, but I take it from her and throw it into the black garbage bin beside the bar.

"You're free to live your life now, Rox. You don't need a cut to define you." I grab her and kiss her passionately, feeling her melt in my arms. I smile into our kiss and I feel like we're young adults again.

"Thank you." She whispers, biting her lip to keep from smiling. There it is – the smile I so badly want to see more of. We make our way out of the bar and I lock it behind me this time, not needing anymore intruders coming in. It's still early in the afternoon, so I've got a few hours to kill before I have to open the bar.

I want to take Rox to see the heart of Port Dover – what this area is known for every Friday the 13th. I follow behind her to find where she parked her bike and I feel my chest tighten seeing our signature bike sitting there, the familiar symbol for the Devil's Rejects sitting on the side. It's not as big as I remember, or maybe Rox decided against picking the larger one that all the men in the club had to have. She tugs me along because I pause nervously upon seeing a bike again, one I'm actually going to get on again.

"Joe, are you okay?" She gives my hand a squeeze and I nod. This time I don't contain the smile that crosses my face. I take a seat on the bike and Rox climbs on behind me, wrapping her arms around me. I put the key in its hole and slowly turn it.

Feeling the rumble, the bike comes to life, vibrating my entire body and sending a jolt of unbreakable joy through me. I let out a loud laugh and kick the stand up.

"You ready?" I turn towards Rox and she shoves a helmet on my head just as I ask. I rest my hand on her thigh as she tightens my helmet so it's secured in place.

"Ready." She knocks my helmet lightly with hers and I smile awkwardly with my cheeks being compressed together in the helmet.

I twist around so I'm facing the front and feel Rox wrap her arms around my torso. She taps my leg to know she's ready, just like she used to in the past. I smile and rev it, shooting us forward onto the street. I let out a loud whoop as we take off in the small town streets. Although I've been hearing the rumble from the bikes all morning, nothing compares to being back on a bike and feeling the vibration under me. I speed past a yellow light and feel Rox laughing behind me, her body shaking against mine. The main strip falls quickly behind me as I head towards Port Dover, about a ten minute drive from Simcoe. I flick my wrist backwards and the bike shoots forward as we head onto the country roads, unable to contain the smile on my face. The feeling of being home overwhelms me. After thirty long years, I'm back on a bike with the woman of my dreams – something I never thought I'd say.

CHAPTER FOUR

ROX

The laughter that comes from Joe brings an overwhelming sense of happiness that I haven't felt in years. His excitement is palpable as he shoots the bike forward, taking every turn to make our ride longer.

It stirs something deep within me that I want to play with. I bite my lip because this feels so familiar, yet so new. I'm not sure if it's because of the years that have passed, but I want to rekindle the past – with the now.

I begin to trail my hand lower towards Joe's cock. When I palm it, I realize it's already hard. I think being on a bike again has stirred up some familiar feelings for him too. I keep moving my hand in an up and down motion, rubbing him torturously over his pants.

One of my favorite parts of being on a bike is the vibration that is constant while riding. I lean my pelvis forward and allow the vibration to send a jolt to my clit.

I moan and palm his erection before we take a sharp turn at an intersection. All I see ahead is vacant farm land, with no house or soul nearby. I keep teasing Joe until he skids the bike to a halt on the side of the road.

"You're fucking kill me, Rox." He growls out and throws his helmet on the ground before flipping himself around. He kicks out the stand and sits backwards with his legs planted to keep the bike upright.

"Stand up, and slide those pants down your legs... slowly." He doesn't break eye contact with me while saying that. I bite my bottom lip and stand up, throwing my leg over the seat to stand beside him. I've always loved him telling me what to do. Any other man? Absolutely not, Joe is the only exception.

I unbutton my jeans and slowly peel them down my legs, bending over so he gets a clear look into my shirt where my breasts sit nestled. I hear the sound of a zipper and stand up to see Joe with his cock in hand, trailing up and down.

"Come here." He demands and I don't bother being mouthy because I want him. I've never felt the need I feel with Joe.

He grabs my hip and with his opposite hand, he bends me over and brings my mouth to his cock.

"Suck." He hisses through his teeth and I do. I stick my tongue out and lick the length of his cock. I smile when I see the tattoo he has there.

"So it's always been mine, huh?" I pause and look at him and he smirks down at me.

"Always." He says before pushing me back down. I take him in my mouth and nothing pleases me more than knowing he never covered up my name tattooed on his cock. If he's been with anyone after me, they had to see another woman's name there knowing he would always belong to me. I lightly graze my teeth and he groans out into the farm filled area.

I continue bobbing my head and jump when I feel his finger sliding between my legs to my lips. I may not have the libido I had as a teenager, but being with Joe reminds my body of its wants and needs.

I begin to move my hips with his finger, but he teases my lips, never inserting a finger. A whimper leaves me with his cock filling my mouth and I pick up the pace. I rest my hands on his thighs and feel them flex, knowing he's close to climaxing.

I moan around him, the vibration of my moan on his cock causes him to grunt as he slides his finger deep inside me. I shiver as the warm sun beats down on my skin. Joe curves his finger in me and I grip his thighs tighter, my knees locking as I try to keep the same momentum on his cock.

"Fuck, Rox." He groans out before exploding and releasing into my mouth. I take everything he gives me, swallowing it as he picks up his pace on my pussy.

I raise my face up, bringing our mouths together as he pumps his fingers deep in me. My toes curl in my boots, and I bite his lip to keep from screaming out as my orgasm plummets through me. My back arches as his fingers keep pumping until I finally feel myself coming back to my senses. I become lax but Joe's not done yet.

"Nah uh, Rox." He leans back, his forearms resting on the handlebars of the bike, "Get on my cock – now." I look down and see he's fully erect again. For a man in his fifties, his stamina clearly hasn't gone anywhere. I honestly don't think it will because, after the time apart, we have a lot of time to make up for.

I throw my leg over the bike and maneuver myself by throwing my legs over his and rising up so the tip of his cock is at my center. I put my hands on his shoulders to support myself and slowly lower myself onto his cock. It feels larger now compared to before when he was on top. We both groan out once I'm fully seated in him.

"Holy fuck, this is… a lot." I say and he throws his head back and laughs. His blue eyes are sparkling with mischief as I slowly begin to move up and down.

Joe leans forward and pulls my shirt down so he can wrap his mouth around one of my tight nipples. He brings his warm mouth to my left nipple and circles the peak slowly, causing me to slam down on him from the tease as he bites down just enough to send a zap of pain that quickly turns pleasurable.

"Oh you're playing dirty, aren't you?" I rise up, just enough that his cock almost slips free, but slam back down and he lets out a guttural noise that I've never heard before.

"Alright, you win. I can't fucking compete when you're wrapping me like silk." He moans as he grabs my neck force-fully and kisses me. Our tongues entwine with one another as I pick up the pace again. I feel his legs straining under mine to keep the bike from toppling over, but that doesn't stop me from quickening my pace. He brings one hand down to my clit and I smile into our kiss.

"I'm close, Rox. I need you to get there too." He begs as I lean down and lick his neck. I place my mouth just under his ear and suck. He lets out a loud growl that we can hear echo around the vacant land. He adds more pressure to my clit and switches directions and begins to play with my clit in circular motions.

"Just like that." I say breathlessly. I feel the familiar tingle begin in my core and my pussy clenches around Joe's cock and finally an orgasm begins to peak. The heavenly feeling flows through me just as Joe lets go and releases into me. We're both glistening from the mixture of sex and heat that surrounds us in the early afternoon sun.

"You still make me feel alive, Rox." Joe admits and I smile, leaning down to give him a soft kiss.

"And you make me feel the same, handsome." I slowly rise from his lap, feeling his cock fall from me and swing my leg over to put my pants back on.

"Do we still have time to go wherever you were planning to take me?" I ask as I wiggle my jeans back up my legs. I secure the button and grab both of our helmets from the ground and hand Joe his.

"I own the bar, I can open it whenever I want... or not." He winks at me and puts his helmet over his head. I laugh and do the same.

We get ourselves situated properly and begin our journey to wherever he's taking me. A detour is never a bad thing, especially when it means I get two orgasms. I hug him tightly from behind as we take off again. The ends of my hair whip around behind me and I take a deep breath. I feel like I'm dreaming.

All I ever wanted in my life was to have these moments. Moments filled with pure utter joy, with Joe at my side.

I squeal as he picks up the pace and takes a sharp turn. We fly through the backroads and I finally see a big sign that says "Welcome to Port Dover". I should have known he was going to bring me here, into the heart of what the area is widely-known for.

We slow down to the speed limit and it doesn't seem like there is much going on.

Maybe it's too early?

He continues driving into what I assume is the main area of the town and I gasp as we make it further in where we see bikes everywhere.

There are bikes parked on both sides of the road, and in the middle. It's like a bikers porno, there's easily over two hundred bikes surrounding the road as we make our way slowly into the heart of it all. I watch as bikers glance at us and my instinct is to squeeze Joe harder around the waist. It's a possessive move, but I don't mind. Bikers are either the nicest people you'll ever meet, or the worst. I've tended to lean towards the latter.

Joe drives us towards what looks like a pier with a small lighthouse at the end and reverses the bike into a tight spot. Some of the bikers' eyes glaze over my bike, making me grimace. If anyone knows the emblem, they may also know who I am.

A guy to our left whistles, "Devil's Rejects from Cali, huh? Long way from home." He smirks as he crosses his legs over one another, leaning on his bike.

"Not far enough." I mutter and Joe snickers in front of me, overhearing me. I hop off the bike and grab both our helmets, locking them into the saddlebags.

"Come on," Joe grabs my hand and we start to walk towards where the eaves are lapping at the wall of the pier. It reminds me of California, except people don't know me here and I don't have to constantly look over my shoulder.

I feel... relaxed. The smell of lake water, fried food, and fish perfumes the air and I take in a lungful of it.

"What are you thinking about, Rox?" Joe nudges my shoulder and I smile. I look up into his face and still can't get over the surrealness of it all. His blue eyes still shine so bright regardless of the disturbances he's been through, and his face has aged – much like mine, but he's still the most handsome man I've ever seen. I always knew that Joe would be one of those men that aged well. When we were teenagers, I used to tease him about it because he had a baby face. Well, he's definitely passed that stage. As much as I wished I was coming to see a beer bellied asshole, I'm much happier seeing Joe like this.

"I'm thinking about how I was right." I say smugly.

"About what?" He questions pulling me towards him, wrapping his arms around me as he leans against the wall of the pier.

"About how you definitely aged well." I laugh and he rolls his beautiful blue eyes. He wraps his arms tightly around me and rests his head on mine.

"I could say the same about you. You still make me want to fall to my knees." He kisses my head and I swoon. I haven't swooned in years, but dammit, Joe has got me feeling all the flutters I felt as a twenty year old.

"Alright enough, this is definitely a place we can't fuck." I laugh, shoving away from him, and he catches me and brings me back.

Leaning down towards my ear he whispers, "Don't tempt me. That's one thing we never got caught doing, I'm sure we still wouldn't." He smirks, a dangerous gleam in his eye. I laugh and push away from him harder this time. We're definitely not teenagers anymore.

"Alright, so tell me, what's with all the bikers? Why do they come here?" I walk backwards, never breaking eye contact. I keep walking until he gives in and follows me. His doc martens thudding on the floor as he trails towards me. I turn just as he reaches me, and he wraps his arm around my shoulder.

"Honestly, it's a weird story. So, there was some guy named Chris in 1981 who was a biker and wanted to get together with his buddies – about twenty or so of them," Joe pauses to nod at a group of men. I'm assuming their locals by their friendly smiles. I guess owning a bar means you probably know a lot of people in the area.

"They got together at a local place here in Port Dover and one of the guys mentioned them doing it every year on the thirteenth of any Friday in the year. As years went on, their get together got larger and larger – and now there are bikers from all over North America that come every time there is a Friday the thirteenth." He motions around and I stare around, amazed.

"So even clubs will come here, and nothing bad will happen?" I ask.

"No, it's pretty peaceful for the most part. There have been some fights that have occurred, but there is plenty of police presence if you haven't noticed." His eyes point towards where a couple cops walk up the small hill to the main strip.

"Interesting…" I've seen a couple different cuts while walking around, some I even recognize from meetings at the clubhouse. It's interesting how they all put their differences aside to come enjoy a time with others who are loyal to bikes.

Joe glances down at his watch and I see a touch of reluctance grace his face.

"What's wrong?" I ask as we stop in line at some place called the Arbor. I see a burly guy at the front window grab a hot dog and my eyes widen seeing how long it is.

"I've got to get back to the bar soon, it's already three o'clock. I'll have customers start trickling in around four after they finish work." He licks his lip, eyeing one of the hot dogs and I can't help but giggle like a schoolgirl. I've never seen a grown man salivate over a hot dog.

"Laugh all you want, but when you try one of these foot-long hot dogs, you'll be the same." He smiles as he wraps his arms around me. We finally make it to the window after fifteen minutes and Joe orders us two hot dogs with the works.

We wait a few minutes before two long ass hot dogs are given to us through a small window. We give our thanks and I stare down at the hot dog that is barely visible under all the toppings.

"Alright, what is this thing?" I ask, bizarrely staring at it as we walk back to my bike. We begin to cross the street and I try to focus on where I'm going, but keep staring down at this thing in my hand. I've seen a lot of things in my fifty years, but never a footlong hot dog covered in literally every topping.

"It's a hot dog, come on, take a bite." He urges me.

"Where do I start? This thing is huge." I laugh trying to bring it to my mouth in different directions. Joe just laughs at me as he leans back, sitting on my bike. I hadn't even realized we made it back to the bike, too preoccupied with my food. It smells delicious, but is definitely intimidating.

I watch Joe practically unhinge his jaw as he wraps his mouth around the hot dog and takes a massive bite. He moans, and I groan, not sure if it's from his noise or because I want to attempt this hot dog.

Alright, fuck it. I open my mouth until I feel my jaw hurt and shove the end into my mouth and chomp down.

"Oh my god," I exclaim with my mouth full.

"You've never been sexier." Joe winks, and I roll my eyes, telling him to fuck off. The taste of fresh bread, sausage, and all the toppings are delicious. I don't say a word as I continue eating while watching people walk by. Some smile and some look at the bike emblem with slight fear in their eyes. I understand the fear; we don't have the best reputation. I mean, who would with a name like Devil's Rejects? Doesn't matter now though, I left that life for good. I spent thirty years basically being my dad's mule, different jobs in different states. He expected me to take over, but everyone knows that a woman doesn't take over a motorcycle club – some long lasting misogynistic rule. However, my dad thought he could change that somehow after years of being the president. He didn't have any family, and he had been a part of the club way before I was even born – or a thought for that matter. Apparently life had a different direction for him too. My dad had a one night stand with someone and they dropped me off as soon as I was born, never looking back. I could have tried to look for her, but why look for someone who clearly didn't want you? My life has always been chaotic, and for once, I was just serene.

I don't know what's in store for me now that I've left California, but I know I want everything removed that gives even a glimpse into my club life. I already feel refreshed not wearing my cut. It had become a second skin, but I'm glad Joe took it out of my hands and threw it in the garbage.

"Want to see what a Friday night is like as a bar owner in a small town?" Joe grabs our helmets from the saddlebag once we finish eating, hands me mine, and tugs his on.

"Please, I'll run circles around you. I used to serve drinks to bikers." I challenge him as I tug my helmet on, tightening it under my chin.

"Alright then – let's go, cocky." He helps me onto the back of the bike and I wrap my arms around him again. Turning on the bike, he lets out the same excited glee as he did earlier today. Joe belongs on a bike. I just don't think he ever expected to go this long without riding one. A glimmer of hope wraps itself around me because I hope I can be the one to ensure he never goes a day without a ride again.

CHAPTER FIVE

JOE

Rox helps me connect the new kegs under the bar and organizes the bar top to suit her. I smile watching her in my bar, tidying things to the way she wants it. I really hope she doesn't plan to leave, she's leaving her mark everywhere. A pang of unease hits me in my gut not knowing the answer to that.

"I'm opening the doors," I shout to her and she hollers for me to open them already and I laugh. Rox has changed so much, but she's still the fiery girl I remember as a young adult. She was always fearless, ready to take anything on, but she had a tad more innocence to her back then compared to now. Now she has a more sexy rugged look to her from years of being in a motorcycle club. That shit will age you quickly.

I walk behind the bar and smack her ass, just as people start to make their way into the bar. I turn on the myriad of TVs around the bar to different sports channels and watch as the place fills up with people finishing work, or just coming in from Port Dover. Over the years, I've built quite a reputation for bikers on this day. Some know about my past, which is why they return to help a fellow "fallen" biker. One of them actually said that to me and I had to reign in my anger. I'm not an angry person, but in that moment, I got angry. I left because I chose to, I could have stayed and gotten myself killed – but I didn't.

"Alright, you didn't lie – it's packed in here." Rox yells over the crowd that's all over the bar. We continue to move in sync as we make drinks and serve them in record time.

"How is it already eight o'clock?" Rox asks, and I laugh as we take a small break. Everyone has got a drink in hand and is enjoying their night.

"Time moves fast when it's busy. I never realize how exhausted I am until I pass out in my bed. I enjoy it though, it's been the one thing to bring me happiness in the thirty years I've been here." I admit and she saddles up beside me and leans her head on my shoulder.

I look towards the door and smile, my girls are here. Well – my girls and Auston, he's now become a part of their group.

"Your eyes just lit up, what's going on?" Rox is gazing up at me and I laugh because she's not wrong.

"My girls and one of her men just walked in. These girls have been coming here since their high school days and haven't stopped. They come visit me all the time. They've become like daughters to me, especially Victoria. She lost her parents while in university," I pause, sadly because I remember how devastated she was when it happened. The girls came into the bar after the funeral and drowned their sorrows in alcohol. I let them because I understood what it was like to lose everything in the blink of an eye.

"I was always here for them, even if it was just wings and beer they wanted." I smile as they make their way towards the bar. Their usual booth is already taken. I wasn't expecting them tonight, so I didn't think to close it off.

"Joe." They all shout in unison and I laugh because it

never gets old. Auston reaches over the bar and we slap each other's hand and I get started on their usuals.

I watch as Victoria's eyes glance over to Rox working behind the bar and she lifts an eyebrow at me and I smirk. I call Rox over and she walks over hesitantly, unsure what the hell I'm about to do.

"Rox, this is Victoria, Auston, Hannah, and Emma." I point at each of them and they all say their hello's with a smile on their faces. I can see Emma's eyes already bouncing back and forth between us trying to figure out our story. The same look is on Victoria's and I laugh.

"Alright, ask away. Your faces aren't hiding a thing." I throw my bar towel over my shoulder and prepare for the bombardment of questions. If it was anyone else asking me questions, I wouldn't give them my time of day. But these kids have become literal kids to me, I look forward to them coming into the bar every week.

"I'm getting the sense that there is a past here..." Emma wags her eyebrows up and down.

"That's not exactly a question." Rox jokes and we all chuckle.

"Who are you?" Victoria blurts and I laugh at that. Victoria used to be this woman who hid in the shadows, behind her friends. Since meeting Auston though, he's opened her up and it makes me happy. Besides them sneaking into my bathroom the odd night to fuck, they are great kids.

"Rox is the only woman I've ever loved." I say sheepishly and the girls gasp.

"Oh you're going to have to say more than that, or these three aren't going to leave you alone." Auston says to Rox and I make a face that says "oops" because he's not wrong. I groan out because the girls have always had a sneaking suspicion about me. I know they know a portion because

Hannah's dad was an officer and he had looked into me all those years ago when I arrived in this small town. He threatened me as soon as he met me, assuming I was bringing ruckus to his town. Little did he know, I was running from it.

I lean forward, placing my elbows on the bar before saying, "As you know, I was in a motorcycle club when I was younger," I pause because they all shout they knew it. It's freaky how similar they all are, and in sync with one another. I shake my head at them and continue, "some nasty stuff went down and I left. Which included leaving Rox behind to deal with the mess I made. However, she recently found me after thirty years and came here to give me shit…" I pause to take a breath of air.

"Oh, oh, let me guess. You guys fell back in love?" Emma swoons and Victoria brings her hands under her chin in hopefulness and I look towards Rox. Her eyes are looking up at mine and some unspoken words cross between us.

"I don't think I ever fell out of love with Rox," I say out loud to no one specifically. Rox smiles and she leans up and kisses me softly on the lips. This simple peck on the lips to them may just seem like a symbol of affection, but to me? It means Rox might actually be reciprocating those feelings back after all these years.

"Okay, here I thought I had the best news ever, but seeing Joe in love tops it," Victoria whispers, and I break apart from Rox. She hugs me tightly before letting go.

"Best news ever?" I question. I didn't even realize they might all have come here to tell me something, too preoccupied with the gorgeous woman at my side all day. I raise an eyebrow at her in question.

Victoria shoots her hand towards me, a beautiful emerald shaped ring gleaming against all the light in the bar. My eyes shoot towards Auston first and he has a huge shit eating grin on his face and I let out a boisterous laugh.

"Congratulations, you two. That is such amazing news." I grab both of their hands and give them a squeeze. The smile on Victoria's face says it all. She doubted herself for so many years, and now she's coming to the realization of what everyone around her has told her for years – she deserves all the light she gives to others.

"I'd say this calls for a round, or ten, of celebratory shots?" Rox lifts a bottle of whiskey in question. Everyone hollers and I roll my eyes. Rox has been here less than a day and she's already winning over people in town. These four kids are some of the only people I really care about in this town though. I feel a gleam of hope in my chest that there might be one more person that I care about becoming permanent in this town. I stare at them all talking as Rox pours shots. She questions Victoria and Auston with the mundane questions about their life. I see behind her biker persona though, she's genuinely immersed in another person's happily ever after because she never got to have the one I promised.

I'm going to change that though because I'm not going anywhere this time – and I hope she's not either.

CHAPTER SIX
ROX

"So, what do you guys all do for a living?" I ask, curiosity peeking as I serve our second round of shots. They all took these shots of whiskey like champs. The three girls definitely made a face of bitterness, but that's not stopping them from celebrating on a Friday night.

"The three of us are teachers and Auston is the principal. We have the summer off, but Auston has been helping his dad for the summer." We all cheers and down the whiskey. Joe's off to the side helping customers, but he takes quick little glances at me throughout to make sure I'm okay. I've survived a lot of years on my own, but nothing feels as good as having someone care for you.

"Oh really? What does he do? Sorry – I don't mean to be nosey." I laugh, and he smiles. A beautiful smile this one has. Definitely a pretty boy, but in a more sophisticated way.

"He's a contractor. He's actually in the process of lining up a contract for a new law firm that wants to branch their firm to Canada. It's for Clare Westminster Woods and Graham VanWinkle – apparently they're some well-known lawyers who want to create an empire of law. They're looking to branch their services across North America and are starting with Toronto." Auston smiles and I'm surprised. His dad seems to be running a successful business that he's not working for full-time. I obviously ask him about that and he mentions how teaching has always been his calling, not building.

I continue to question them about their lives, until Joe brings out a platter of steaming wings that smell delicious.

"Did you make those?" He mentions Jacob, the worker in the back, made them as I quickly steal one from the platter and take a huge bite, moaning at the barbecue sauce that hits my senses.

Fuck, this is delicious after a long night of making drinks.

I take a few more bites until I'm done, finishing off with a moan. I look up to catch Joe staring at me with a feral look in his eyes.

His eyes darken as I lick the sauce off my fingers, slowly. I purposely tease him, seeing how far I can take it. I see the inner battle in his eyes – and the moment his restraint breaks.

He walks over and hoists me over his shoulder and mumbles to the other bartenders that he will be back shortly. I laugh and look up to see the four kids looking up at us with surprise in their eyes. I'm guessing they never got to see this playful, lustrous, side of Joe that I did years ago.

"Where are we going?" I muse and Joe shoves open the freezer door and the blast of cold makes me shiver. What the

—

"Not so cocky now, are we?" Joe sets me down on a few of the stacked crates and pushes my legs open so he can stand between them.

"Depends on what you're about to do..." I tease and he chuckles lightly before he grabs my face and brings our mouths together in a frenzy.

I will never get enough of this man, or his cock.

He runs his hands down my sides until he has a hold of my legs and hoists me up again, this time right side up. He pushes me against the wall as he begins to leave little love bites along my collar and the top of my breast. I moan loudly at the sensation of the coolness from the wall on my back, and the heat of his mouth.

"More," I moan as I reach down to take my shirt off. Joe moves for a minuscule moment before he tugs my shirt down to praise my nipples. They peak at the cold air and friction that Joe is giving me against my pussy. He's slowly rubbing his clothed cock against my center and I feel myself beginning to move with him.

"Stop teasing me and give me your cock. I've spent enough years without it – I need it now." I practically demand as I let out a shuddered breath. I feel him smile as he leaves one last, more painful than the others, love bite. I look down and notice he's left a few scattered around my neck.

He sets me down long enough to chuck both of our pants off. Before picking me back up though, he tugs forcefully on the panties I put on before we came down to the bar for the night and they rip against my body. The force from the tug against my clit leaves me gasping as a shot of pleasure resonates through my body.

"Fuck you're sexy, now wrap those legs around me." He lifts me up so that our cores are aligned and slowly inches forward. I let out a moan as he roughly shoves himself into me after getting the tip in. Letting out a guttural moan, he takes a moment for both of us to adjust to the sensations.

I can't believe after all these years, he still feels this fucking good.

"Move, please." I beg and begin to move my hips in small juts. He takes note and begins to push deep thrusts into me. I grab onto his neck and bring his face to mine, giving him a passionate kiss. I break our kiss and trail my tongue along his jaw, until I reach his ear lobe. From what I remember, this was a sensitive spot for him. I begin to tease around the area with my tongue and feel his grip tighten on my thighs. The grip is enough to leave a bruise, which tells me that this spot is still indeed, his sensitive spot.

"Fuck," He grits out. "I won't last long with you doing that, Rox." He breathes as I move my head away, bringing our eyes back together. I bite my bottom lip and reach my hand down between us to play with my clit. His thrusts begin to speed up, and I apply more pressure and motion on my clit. The familiar tingle begins at my toes and travels upwards until I explode around him.

"Fuck, Joe." I groan out as I dig my nails into his neck. His thrusts become erratic as he reaches his own peak.

"Fuck." He grinds out in the space between my neck and shoulder. I loosen my arms around him slightly and rest my head on his.

"You okay?" I ask while rubbing his arms and he huffs out a laugh. He leans back, keeping a hold of me, but looks into my eyes with so much hope and love that it makes my eyes tear up.

"How long are you staying?" Joe runs his finger down my face, fear etched in his eyes now that he's asked the big question. I wait a few moments to build some suspense – knowing it will be making his stomach turn.

"Indefinitely – if you still want me." The smile that crosses his face is better than anything I've seen in my life. His eyes light up and for the first time in twenty years, I feel like I belong. I belong in the arms of the man I fell in love with almost forty years ago, until the day I die.

EPILOGUE
JOE

Two months later...

I stare out at the sun setting as I stand on the pier in Port Dover. It's a Sunday evening in September and it's serene here. Nobody is walking around which makes it almost perfect.

What would make it perfect is the moment I see Rox, my soon-to-be wife, walking towards me.

"How do you feel?" Auston asks beside me and I laugh, unable to hold it in.

"I've been waiting thirty plus years to call Rox my wife. I'm glad the moment you realized you wanted Victoria to be your wife, you asked her without second thoughts. My biggest regret is not making her my wife and bringing her with me all those years ago." I stare out into the water as I say that and I look to Auston and see a sad smile on his face.

"Well, it looks like you've got some time to make up for it then. I know nothing can make the pain of all those years go away, but life's giving you a second chance. It's best not to waste it when everything you want is right in front of you." Auston smirks as he says that last part and I turn to see Rox walking towards me in a black lace dress that hits her mid-thigh, doc martens, and a bouquet of red flowers that match her lips. Beside her walks Victoria.

We asked Auston and Victoria to be our witnesses since we didn't have much choice in people. I don't think we made a bad choice though because the joy vibrating off of them is palpable.

"You look fucking gorgeous, Rox." I smile and she returns it. I can feel her giddiness as she comes up beside me and turns towards the officiant. The standard words are said, but before we sign any papers, I interrupt the officiant.

"I know we said we weren't going to do any vows, but fuck it, I'm doing it. Rox – I never thought I was going to see you again. My biggest regret in life was leaving you behind to fight my battles when I knew I couldn't face them. I can list off all the things I regret in my life, but instead I'm going to say what I'm most grateful for – you. The moment you walked into my bar, with anger and resentment in your eyes, I knew I had to fix things. Not for me though, for you. You deserved a life full of love and happiness, something I promised to give you and didn't. I hope I can make up for it now though. We've got lots of time ahead of us, and I don't want to waste a moment of it away from you ever again." I look up because fuck, I've got tears in my eyes after opening up to Rox. I look back down at her, and she has tears streaming down her beautiful face.

"I love you so fucking much." She sniffles as Victoria quickly passes her and me a tissue. The officiant smiles as he asks us to say our "I dos" and pronounces us husband and wife.

"I told you one day I would marry you under the sunset." I bring her lips to mine and bend her backward. I hear Victoria and Auston holler behind us, and nothing beats this feeling. Although it took thirty years for this moment, it's better late than never.

Although, I don't think never was ever an option because life always has a way of bringing the things you love back to you.

Want to read Auston and Victoria's story? Here's a sneak peek at *Hot for the Principal*, available now!

A sexy
contemporary
romance

Hot
for the
PRINCIPAL

ALEXANDRIA GONCALVES

CHAPTER ONE

G *atsby was a loner who didn't deserve Daisy, so his death was kind of deserving.*

That's it?

How can a student end their essay for their grade twelve academic English paper like that? How do students think they are going to survive in university ending an essay like that? I remind myself that the question was to state if *The Great Gatsby* was an outdated novel, or if it was still relevant today. Overall confusion dawns on me, as I try to make sense of this student's conclusion.

I put the paper down on my desk and rub my temples. How did I end up here? In my hick hometown? As a high school English teacher? I lean back in my chair and thank God that lunch is about to start.

The bell rings signaling to everyone that it's lunchtime. I don't have class during the period before lunch, so I usually spend that time marking students' work… or on Netflix watching *Friends*.

I stand up to disinfect the students' desks, as I do every morning, but I've made it a habit to do so during lunch as well because everyone is getting sick. With the beautiful winter in Ontario, students are sicker than usual, especially since exam season starts next week. I go around the thirty desks to make sure they're somewhat clean and put the spray back in the brown cupboards that usually stay locked.

I look around the room and sigh. The walls are all off-white bricks with a blackboard taking up a full side, well almost—there is an active board that sits in the middle. What was once just a simple chalkboard has now become a large screen that projects my computer screen to students. It also allows me to write on it, like a chalkboard. Instead of chalk I use a pen that connects to the special surface of the smart board. On the opposite side of the smart board there are windows. Some classrooms at Angel's Catholic High School don't have them, but thankfully mine does. I open up the bland grey covers and allow a small amount of sunshine to come through. My desk sits near the door and shows a little glimpse of who I'm to my students. I have a pencil holder that looks like a typewriter and a framed photo of me with my two best friends; Hannah and Emma. I walk back over to my desk while straightening a few of the desks along the way.

"Hey babe!" My best friend Hannah walks in with a spring in her step and plants herself on the desk in front of mine. Hannah and I have been friends since grade nine. We have been stuck together since our first day of high school and that was eons ago. Appearance-wise Hannah is my polar opposite, but we're utterly compatible on the emotional front. I'm five-foot-five, with long brown hair that hits the middle of my back, hazel eyes, and a bronze skin tone. With caramel blonde hair, blue eyes and white skin, she's practically a model, standing over me at a stunning six feet. She could definitely be a model if her dream wasn't to be an artist.

"Hey, how was Art class?" I reach under my large, square

49

brown desk and grab my bag. Pulling out my Greek salad, I lean back in my chair and put my feet up.

"You know what, I think these students are finally starting to get it. It's grade nine, so I don't expect them to be fantastic but this one girl, Joana? I can see her becoming an artist. She does beautiful work."

"Well, I'm glad you're hopeful for your students. I had a student end their grade twelve paper like this." I shuffle through the mass of papers on my desk and hand her over the essay. I watch her eyes scan the conclusion, and she spits out her coffee, laughing. Luckily, the spray of liquid missed the papers on my desk. I open the top drawer of my desk and grab wipes to clean off the coffee that was sprayed everywhere.

"Oh my God Vic, I actually feel bad for you. Teaching English is definitely not easy..." She looks at me, sympathetically, and I roll my eyes.

"How did I end up becoming a teacher? In my country-ass hometown?" I ask, throwing my body back and feeling my chair almost tip. I always wanted to be a writer, and I know I still can be. I have all summer to try writing a novel, but as soon as I'm in front of a computer or have my writing book in hand; I freeze. My anxiety gets the best of me, and I end up just putting everything aside and telling myself I'll write my book the next summer.

Four years later, that notebook still sits in my bag. Blank.

Every. Single. Day.

"Oh babe, we live in a competitive world...I always assumed I would be an artist with my work hanging in some beautiful art gallery, but apparently life had different plans." Hannah crosses her legs and shrugs. I continue eating my salad when I hear squeaky running shoes coming down the hallway.

Here comes Emma, the last of our trio. Emma is naturally beautiful with short black hair, brown eyes, and an olive skin tone. I love Emma because we're both short, which makes us feel better when we're standing next to Hannah. The three of us became inseparable in tenth grade when Emma moved to Simcoe from Edmonton. Although Hannah and I had already been friends, Emma's magnetism drew us to her on the first day of tenth grade. It was a dramatic change, but she made friends with the perfect girls.

"Oh, my God! Sorry for being late, some boy thought he could lift more than he could handle and ended up with the barbell coming down on his forehead. It was a disaster, I just took him to the office to head home." She takes a pause and sits down beside Hannah. "Why do boys think showing off is a good idea? Especially in Gym class? As if you're not six feet tall, sexy, and all man… you're fifteen, five-foot-five, and your balls haven't even dropped!" I laugh, I can't help it. This is why I love Emma. She doesn't hold back, but she's a ray of sunshine on a shitty day. We continue to talk about our day, and then suddenly, Emma slams her hands down on her desk.

"I forgot to tell you guys, Principal Hiffin put in her notice for retirement. She won't be back for next semester!" Hiffin is an elderly woman who has been a principal for over twenty-five years. She could be mean, but if you got on her good side, then you were all good. Even at twenty-nine years old, I'm still afraid of principals… especially since she was mine.

"What? But we're just getting to exams for the first semester. How are they supposed to find a principal in the middle of the year?" I ask Emma. She always has all the answers. She's the one you go to when you want a good laugh and the inside scoop on everything going on in these brick walls. Last year she caught two teachers going at it in the boys' locker room - after school hours, of course. It was still no less of a shock. Emma didn't tell anyone except us, but eventually, the fuck buddies got caught...and lost their positions. You would think teachers would know not to mess around with one another.

"Well, allegedly they already found one. He will be coming in from the city and apparently, he's a hard ass. Doesn't really like to socialize and keeps to himself." Lucky him, I think, wondering if he will be able to talk his way out of going to the bar on Friday night. Every Friday after school, all the teachers go to Kline's, a local bar, for drinks. The girls and I always try to get out of it.

Emphasis on *try*.

"Is he another old person? I swear it's so difficult to keep the older staff up to date on all the latest technology we use." Hannah groans; she's not just good at Art, she's also a tech wiz. Which is why she's always called in to help the older teachers when they can't get their computers to turn on. I laugh to myself, remembering the time that one of our colleagues unplugged his computer with his foot. He would have thrown the damn thing on the ground if it wasn't for Hannah coming in and plugging it back in.

"Apparently not..." Emma takes a bite of her ham sandwich and continues on with her mouth full, "From what I know he's only thirty-three, a total hard ass for rules, but sexy as hell. I haven't seen him, but that's what I've heard..." She shrugs. I'm curious as to where Emma gets all her information from. She loves participating in extracurriculars; nothing that has changed from when we were students. She frequently attends conventions and meets with various teachers around Ontario. It came to benefit us as she would get all the scoop from one side of the province to the other.

"Now I'm intrigued, I can't wait until after exams to find out for ourselves!" Emma smirks and pretends to swoon. I roll my eyes at her. All three of us are almost thirty and single. We would go out and meet men, but in a town of four-teen-thousand people, most already have families or are elderly; the pond is limited. I close my glass container and put it back in my bag. Emma throws hand sanitizer my way, and I put a small circle in my hands. The strong smell of alcohol and flowers filling the air. Emma tries her best to mask the smell of sweaty teenagers with the highly fumigated hand sanitizer.

"Do you have your exams ready, Vic? They start tomor-row, right?" Emma asks me, and I nod.

"Yes, they do, thank God." I take my legs off my desk and stand up to stretch. I feel the pull between my shoulders, giving me release from sitting for over three hours. I should consider moving around more during my lessons. "Then I will be marking until Friday, and then long weekend!" I do a little shake of my hips. This is one of my favorite times of the year, usually on long weekends teachers have to stay up marking. This year, however, the exams will be over before the long weekend which means we can actually spend our time relaxing before the new semester.

The bell rings and our girl time is over. Emma grimaces, knowing her next period is grade twelve Fitness. Which means it's a mixture of people who may not want to be there but need a Gym credit; the perks of a high school curriculum.

I wave the girls goodbye and go to the front of the class-room to erase the notes from my earlier class. I hate having to use this pen to erase things. I have to click the little eraser icon on the screen and drag it along the plastic material. The scratching sound of the pen dragging is worse than nails on a chalkboard. My shoulders slump due to my last period being grade ten English. These students don't have a care in the world for school. I prefer teaching grade eleven and twelve because at least they make an effort with their studies. After all, post-secondary is only a couple years away.

The classroom becomes louder as students filter into their seats. Every student has a phone now, and it makes teaching so tricky. If you take away a student's phone, you become a "bitch," but if you don't take it away, they're distracted the entire time.

"Good afternoon guys, if you could put your phones away that would be appreciated. I don't want to have to take it away, but if I notice it becoming a problem; it's gone." I pause to watch some nod their heads, and some roll their eyes. "We're almost done with the semester, just a few more things to go over. I will be giving you guys the rest of the class to study for your final exam that's coming up." I walk over to the computer and start the final review slide of the term.

"Oh my God, finally!" I say aloud to myself. It's finally three o'clock, and school is over. I thought I dreaded this more when I was a teenager, but it's so much worse as a teacher. I want to get out of here and have an evening to myself before I have to be here again tomorrow morning. I grab my bag from underneath my desk and throw it over my shoulder.

Locking my door, I head towards the front doors to the parking lot. These hallways always leave me anxious. I try to walk as fast as my heels will take me to get out of here. People always liked to say, "You're going to miss high school and university, they're some of the best days of your life" and I still disagree with that statement. School was my worst nightmare come to life; there is nothing that could make me go back.

At all.

I step outside into the bright sun which is shining at the end of January, I cannot believe it. Anyone who lives in Canada knows that it's almost always snowing in January. There is snow on the ground, but not enough that I have to wear a full snowsuit and boots to work. I make my way to my black Mini Cooper parked in the staff lot. Trying not to wipe out on the ice as I walk around my car to the driver's side as I try to keep my heels from gliding against the thawing. I unlock my car, open my door, and slide down into the faux leather seats. I throw my beautiful black leather shoulder bag onto the passenger seat and turn the car on. Maluma's *Mala Mía* starts blasting through the stereo, nearly giving me a heart attack. Music is part of what keeps me alive, so I tend to have it blaring at any time of the day.

I put the car in reverse and pull out of my spot to head home. I can't believe another term has gone by, a time of the year that always leaves me feeling anxious and excited. A new semester means new students, fresh minds at work, and more assignments to work on. I roll to a halt at the stop sign near my house and feel my phone vibrate beside me in my bag. I look in my rear view mirror and see nobody behind me, so I grab my phone.

Hannah: So once exams are over, drinks at DP on Saturday?

Me: Absolutely! Emma coming too?

Hannah: Duh!

I'm about to answer back when a sleek black BMW pulls up behind me. I can't see the person behind the wheel to gauge if they're irritated or not.

I take my foot off the break and throw my phone back on the seat. I turn left towards my house and drive for another eight minutes before pulling up my driveway. I live on the outskirts of Simcoe, just far enough to be away from people, but close enough that I don't dread running errands or my drive to work.

I pull up to my house. It's a beautiful, simple rustic country bungalow with large glass windows framed by wood pieces that make them pop. Most country homes have a wrap around porch, but mine has a multi-stone square porch in front of the French doors. My porch would be much larger if I didn't have a swing bed installed, but I wanted to be able to sit in my front yard comfortably because it's where the sun sets. I saw the idea for the bed swing on Pinterest and had our local contracting company come in and install it. It's the perfect place to sit on a beautiful day.

I park my car in the separate garage and grab my bag on the way out. One thing I hate about this house is the independent garage. The snow and I aren't friends, so the trek isn't ideal especially since I wear heels ninety percent of the time. I walk carefully, dodging the ice on the driveway while closing the garage. I reach the French doors and unlock one. Throwing the door open, I kick off my heels as I walk in and throw my bag on the lavender ottoman sitting against the wall in the foyer.

This house used to be so different. Save for the swing, the exterior of my house has always been the same. Once it became mine, I had some walls knocked down, the walls repainted, and I revamped the master bedroom, kitchen, and laundry room. Emma and Hannah love coming over because of how big and rustic everything looks.

I put my containers in the dishwasher and grab a bottle of wine out of the fridge. The next two days are full of exams, so I will be marking for what is going to feel like a year. I take a big gulp from my glass of wine and get ready for the upcoming exam season.

ACKNOWLEDGMENTS

Thank you to:

My fiancé, for always supporting my wild passion for everything romance.

My amazing friends Jessi, Bri, Willow, and Sophie for helping me bring this to life with your excitement, feedback, and love.

Thank you to Nisha Ladlee for taking on my project and helping to make it shine.

Writing this has been a whirlwind of a journey. I hope you take the time to review my novel, let me know what you think (critical feedback is always welcome), and take the chance on my future work.

ABOUT THE AUTHOR

Alexandria Goncalves is from a small city in Southwestern Ontario, where she resides with her fiancé. Her passion for writing came at a young age and she found romance novels to help cope with the downsides in life. She pursued an undergrad in English Literature to help improve her writing skills and prepare for a career in writing. She writes a variety of romance that ranges from contemporary to dark and taboo—and everything in between. When she's not focused on her writing, she's nose deep into a book, spending time with her fiancé, posting on her Instagram or TikTok, or laughing with friends. Visit her website at www. authoralexandriagoncalves.com.

instagram.com/authoralexandriagoncalves

Made in the USA
Las Vegas, NV
06 March 2022

45143700R00042